# PRIMA BALLERINA

SCHOLASTIC INC.
New York   Toronto   London   Auckland   Sydney
Mexico City   New Delhi   Hong Kong

Used under license by Scholastic Inc. Published by Scholastic Inc. SCHOLASTIC and associated logos are trademarks and/or registered trademarks of Scholastic Inc.

TM & © Copyright 2010 by OHC Group LLC. All Rights Reserved

ISBN: 978-0-545-16762-8

www.onlyheartsclub.com

12 11 10 9 8 7 6 5 4 3 2 1                    10 11 12 13 14 15/0

Printed in China                    62
First printing, January 2010

The Only Hearts Girls™ formed the Only Hearts Club® in a bond of true friendship. They are a fun-loving bunch of friends who are always there for one another. They laugh, share secrets, and have the greatest adventures together. Most importantly, they encourage one another to listen to their hearts and do the right thing.

*K*arina Grace was in the best mood ever. She was at ballet practice when her teacher pulled her aside to tell her that she had been chosen to perform a solo routine in her dance school's upcoming recital.

A ballet solo! Karina could hardly believe her ears! She loved to dance more than almost anything in the world, and now she felt like all her hard work and practice had truly paid off. Karina would be twirling and whirling in the spotlight for all her friends and family to see. She couldn't wait to tell the rest of the Only Hearts Club.

# Prima Ballerina

Karina didn't have to wait long to tell them. When her Only Hearts Club friends came to pick her up after ballet practice, she blurted out the good news. "I've been given a ballet solo in my dance recital!" she cried.

"Karina, that's amazing!" said Taylor Angelique.

Olivia Hope clapped her hands together in excitement. "We're so happy for you!" she exclaimed. The other girls enthusiastically agreed.

"The recital is next Saturday," Karina said. "That's only two weeks away. I'll have to practice extra hard to get my routine perfect for the show."

"Don't worry, Karina," said Briana Joy. "You're so talented. This performance will be a piece of cake!"

When the girls left the dance studio, they walked toward Lily Rose's house. The girls were having a sleepover. Everyone except for Hannah Faith was coming.

"I wish I could come to the sleepover tonight!" said Hannah. "But I've got a gymnastics meet early tomorrow morning."

"We'll miss you!" said Anna Sophia.

"I'll miss you guys too," said Hannah. "But I was hoping we could do something special for my birthday next week."

"That sounds like fun!" said Kayla Rae. "Good luck at your meet tomorrow!"

The girls waved good-bye to Hannah as she walked off to her house.

At the sleepover that night, the girls were bummed that Hannah wasn't there. But they still had a blast playing games, painting their nails, telling funny stories, and playing with their dogs, who had also been invited to the sleepover. They even let Lily's little sister, Jessica, join them before she went to bed.

Suddenly, Taylor piped up, "I just got the best idea."

"What's up?" asked Karina.

"We should have a surprise birthday party for Hannah next Friday!" Taylor said. "We could make it an amazing day for her."

"Hannah would love that!" said Anna. "I'll bake the cake."

"I'll be in charge of decorations," said Kayla.

The girls were so excited about their surprise birthday party idea. It was perfect!

While the girls spoke excitedly about the party, Karina sat quietly. She was a little worried. This party sounded like fun, Karina thought, but it wasn't nearly as important as her dance performance. She decided she wasn't about to let some party get in the way of preparing for her big solo on Saturday night.

The next morning, the girls planned out their day while having breakfast in Lily's kitchen. While eating cereal and muffins and drinking fresh-squeezed orange juice, they chatted about going to the park.

But Karina couldn't stay. She had to rush off to the studio to practice. So she quickly polished off a muffin, took a gulp of orange juice, and rushed to gather up her things.

"Bye girls!" she said, waving. "I'll talk to you later about planning for Hannah's surprise party."

"Bye Karina!" her friends called. "Don't practice too hard!"

# Prima Ballerina

After a long day of perfecting her solo routine, Karina was exhausted. She went home and plopped down on her bed, ready to get some rest.

Suddenly, her phone rang. It was Olivia calling.

"Hey, K!" said Olivia. "A bunch of us were going to get together tomorrow to plan Hannah's party. We'd love your thoughts on what kind of music to play at the party. Can you come?"

Karina paused. She wanted to help give Hannah a great surprise party, but what was most important to Karina was her dance performance. She had been planning to practice again tomorrow.

"I'd love to," said Karina. "But I have to practice. Maybe I can put together the playlist myself and bring it the day of the party?"

A few days later at the dance studio, Karina was so caught up in her dance routine that she didn't even see her friends wander in to watch.

"Bravo!" they all clapped as Karina triumphantly finished her dance.

"Oh my gosh!" said Karina, surprised to see her friends. "Hey, you guys!"

"Your dance looks amazing," said Hannah. "You can tell you've been working really hard!"

"I want it to be just right," said Karina. "I don't want to let anyone down."

Briana shook her head. "You won't let anyone down. You're going to be fantastic."

"Yeah," echoed Lily. "Why don't you take a break from practicing and come with us for a picnic at the park?"

"Maybe next time," said Karina. "Today I just need to work on my pirouettes a little bit more."

Karina's friends shrugged. "All right. Talk to you later!" they called as they left the studio.

At the park, the Only Hearts Girls—minus Karina—were enjoying their delicious picnic lunch. The girls' dogs, Patches, Dotcom, Sniff, Longfellow, Cupcake, and Bubulina, chased each other and played.

"I'm a little worried about Karina," Kayla said. "She's taking this performance so seriously."

Taylor nodded. "I just hope all of her practicing isn't taking the fun out of her solo," she said.

"I know what to do!" Briana chimed in. "Let's write her a note to tell her how great we think she's doing. Maybe it'll help her realize she doesn't have to worry so much!" Everyone thought that was a perfect idea.

As they were packing up their things to leave the park, Anna pulled Briana aside so that Hannah wouldn't hear. "I hope Karina isn't too busy to make it to Hannah's surprise party tomorrow," she said quietly. "And I hope she does her part and gets that playlist done!"

"Oh, I'm sure she'll be there and she'll put together the best playlist ever," Briana whispered back. "The Only Hearts Club and her friends mean the world to Karina."

# Prima Ballerina

The next day, Karina came home from dance practice to find the note from her friends in her mailbox. It was made with pretty pink paper, glitter glue, and lots of sparkly stickers. All her friends had signed it with sweet notes of encouragement. Karina took a deep breath and smiled, but the note made her even more nervous.

"See, they all know how important this performance is too," she said to herself. "And they're all going to be watching me on Saturday, along with my parents and everyone else."

Hannah's surprise party was that evening and Karina hadn't even finished her playlist yet. She had come home to get that done and then make sure she was at the party on time. However, it was Karina's last day before the performance, and she still didn't feel like everything in her routine was perfect. She didn't have to be at the party for a few hours. *Maybe I should go back and work on a few more things*, she thought. The playlist wouldn't take long. She could get in a little bit more practice, make the perfect playlist, and still make it to the party on time if she hurried.

# Prima Ballerina

Soon, Karina was back at the dance studio, working on her routine again. *I'll only be here for a few minutes, just to work on a couple of little things,* she thought to herself as she worked on a tricky spin.

Karina danced and danced, but she was not satisfied. She started to get a little frustrated, so she kept on practicing. She performed the routine over and over as time flew by.

Finally Karina took a break and looked up at the clock. It was almost seven o'clock! Hannah's surprise party had started at six! Karina had been so focused on her dancing that she had completely forgotten about the party. She was so embarrassed! There was no way she could go to the party this late. She was still in her dance clothes and she hadn't even made the party playlist. She had let everyone down. Her friends would probably hate her now!

The next day was the day of Karina's recital. But that morning, instead of feeling excited or nervous, she felt completely terrible. She knew she should call her friends to apologize, but she just couldn't face them. She hadn't just let down Hannah—she'd let down the entire Only Hearts Club by being so self-centered. The phone rang all morning, but Karina didn't answer it. She just sat quietly, even when her Dalmatian, Dotcom, snuggled close to make sure she was okay. She knew her friends were mad at her. Why wouldn't they be? She had been so selfish for the last couple of weeks, rehearsing nonstop for her solo and spending hardly any time with them, not to mention missing the party. Who knew if they'd even come to her performance that night?

Karina didn't know how to apologize to her friends for what she had done, and she was too embarrassed to call them. So she went to the bookstore and bought Hannah a birthday gift. It was a book about Hannah's favorite gymnast. Karina knew Hannah would love it—she just wished she had remembered to get it in time for the party.

Karina went home and wrapped the book in sparkly wrapping paper. She had already picked out a birthday card that had red hearts inside. She hoped the hearts would show Hannah how special she and the Only Hearts Club were to Karina.

Next, she sat down at her computer. She put together a play-list of all of her favorite songs that reminded her of the Only Hearts Club and her friends. There were happy songs, silly songs, and sad songs—songs that reminded her of the many ups and downs she and her best friends had shared throughout the years.

Then, Karina copied eight CDs—one for each of her best friends, and one for herself. She knew it wasn't much, but she hoped the gesture would help show her friends how sorry she felt.

Meanwhile, the rest of the Only Hearts Girls were spending time together at the mall. But they weren't enjoying themselves because they were so worried about Karina. They hadn't heard from her since before the party.

"I'm sure everything is okay," said Lily. "She probably just got caught up at rehearsal or something like that."

Hannah nodded, "I'm sure you're right. I just hope she knows I'm totally not upset that she missed the party. If *all* of you guys had forgotten my birthday, I might have been upset. But I had so much fun!"

"Well," said Briana, "I can't wait for all of us to show up at the recital tonight and show Karina how much she means to us."

"Hey!" Taylor interjected, suddenly stopping at a case full of pretty charm necklaces. "Check out this necklace. It's a little sparkly bow! It will match Karina's dance costume perfectly! We should totally get it for Karina to show her how much we care about her, and how proud we are of her dancing."

The girls smiled at one another. It was a perfect idea.

# Prima Ballerina

Karina's stomach was full of butterflies as she waited backstage for her performance. A million thoughts were running through her mind. What if she forgot her routine? What if she tripped and fell? What if her friends were so mad, they didn't show up to watch her dance?

Karina decided to take a peek through the curtains. There, in the audience, were all seven of the other Only Hearts Girls, including Hannah, waiting patiently for Karina to take the stage.

Karina smiled. After everything, her friends were there to support her. Her friends couldn't be that mad! Suddenly, she felt calm and ready to perform. When her music cued up, Karina took to the stage and gracefully danced her solo. It was the best performance of her life. When the song was over, Karina posed with a flourish, grinning from ear to ear.

As she curtsied, Karina caught her friends' eyes in the audience. They were clapping and cheering louder than anyone else.

After the show was over, Karina rushed to find her friends. The first thing she did was run over and hug Hannah. Then a rush of words spilled out. "I'm so sorry about missing your birthday," Karina said. "I was so focused on myself and my dance performance that I lost track of time practicing and missed your party. I got too wrapped up in dance, and I totally let you down. I should have been there for you—for all of you. Missing the party and forgetting to put together a playlist was completely against everything the Only Hearts Club stands for, and I promise it'll never happen again."

"It's okay, Karina!" said Hannah. "I know how much this performance meant to you. We all do. I mean, if I had a super important ice-skating performance or a tough gymnastics meet, I'd probably feel exactly the way you did. I know you didn't miss my party on purpose and I forgive you. Hey, you're one of my best friends!"

"Well, thanks," said Karina. "I know it's a little late, but here's your birthday present, Hannah. And I made each of you a CD with songs that remind me of you and how special I think our friendship is."

"Thanks, Karina!" the girls said.

28

"Now we have something for you, too," Hannah said, handing her a small wrapped package.

"We think you're the best ballerina there is," Lily said. "We hope you like it."

Karina opened the package with the little necklace inside. The sparkly bow charm glinted in the light. "Oh my gosh," Karina said. "It's beautiful!"

She smiled at her friends. "I'm so lucky to have friends as wonderful as you."

Karina gave each one of her friends a huge hug. Her performance that night had been practically perfect. But that hardly seemed to matter now. At that moment, Karina just felt so lucky that her friends understood her, and that they accepted her for exactly who she was—mistakes and all.

"Now that we've got you back to ourselves, you want to go out and grab some milkshakes? We can call it my 'after birthday party'!" Hannah teased.

"That sounds great!" said Karina. "You guys are the best, most understanding friends in the world, especially when I wasn't being a very good friend. You really showed me how much you care about me, and reminded me what the Only Hearts Club is all about—listening to your heart and doing the right thing."

# About the Only Hearts Club

Only Hearts Club® is a fashion doll brand that delivers a wholesome and positive image and message to girls. The eight ethnically diverse, soft, poseable dolls feature amazing detail, and look and dress like real girls, in age-appropriate fashions. The brand's message, delivered through a series of Only Hearts Club books, is to "listen to your heart and do the right thing." This image and message are unique.

As detailed in their books, the Only Hearts Girls share the interests and experiences of real girls, such as horseback riding. The Only Hearts Horse & Pony Club is a complete equestrian line featuring soft and poseable horses, dolls in riding outfits, and stables.

The Only Hearts Girls™ also have lots of fun at sleepovers and babysitting their younger siblings, the Only Hearts Li'l Kids™.

The other interests of the members of the Only Hearts Club® include dancing, ballet, sports such as soccer, arts and crafts, cooking and baking, and exploring the outdoors.

They love the tiny, adorable Only Hearts Pets™, like Buddy. Turn the page to learn more about the cutest little animals you've ever seen!

**Girls and parents love the Only Hearts Club:**

*"Thank you for making such wonderful dolls that are a better alternative and teach better values to girls."*

*"It's nice that someone is making dolls that are so much like me."*

*"Thank you for making dolls that are young and sweet, just like my children."*

*"I love, love, LOVE your dolls! Your books are wonderful too!"*

**Available at TARGET stores and specialty toy and gift stores nationwide.**

**www.OnlyHeartsClub.com**

"I make great milkshakes!"

"You've got me by the tail!"

"Dreams can come true!"

"I'm hip and I love to hop!"

"Rise and shine!"

# Only Hearts Pets

- Amazingly cute, tiny plush pets!
- Over 50 styles! Collect them all!
- Great charms for backpacks & bags!
- Sold at Target, Justice & Bed Bath & Beyond!

"Wool you please be my friend?"

"I'm not a boar!"

"I'm purr-fect for you!"

"I love to monkey around!"

"I'm purr-fect for you!"

"Let's horse around!"

"Let's get warm and fuzzy!"

"Gimme some peanuts!"

"I want a bear hug!"

"Maybe I will and maybe I won't!"

"I'm on the loose!"

King

"I'm the mane man!"

Buddy

"Best friends forever!"

Honey

"Oh, how sweet it is!"

Jake

"I'll go get it!"

Silver

"I'm a fancy feline!"

# So small
# Only 2" Tall

Zippy

"I look great in stripes!"

Barkley

"I'm all ears!"

## The cutest things you've ever seen!

Wags

"I'm begging to be with you!"

Blizzard

"The ice is twice as nice!"

Milkshake

"Let's stay with each-udder!"

Boss

"I'm the 800 pound gorilla!"

Stretch

"The sky's the limit!"

Tabby

"I'm the cat's meow!"

Waddles

"I'm always cool!"

Ozzie

"Don't stick your head in the sand!"

Funky

"I love to monkey around!"